Cora and the Elephants

Cora
and
the Elephants

Story by Lissa Rovetch

Art by Lissa Rovetch and Martha Weston

Viking

VIKING
Published by the Penguin Group
Penguin Books USA Inc., 375 Hudson Street, New York, New York 10014, U.S.A.
Penguin Books Ltd, 27 Wrights Lane, London W8 5TZ, England
Penguin Books Australia Ltd, Ringwood, Victoria, Australia
Penguin Books Canada Ltd, 10 Alcorn Avenue, Toronto, Ontario, Canada M4V 3B2
Penguin Books (N.Z.) Ltd, 182–190 Wairau Road, Auckland 10, New Zealand

Penguin Books Ltd, Registered Offices: Harmondsworth, Middlesex, England

First published in 1995 by Viking, a division of Penguin Books USA Inc.

1   3   5   7   9   10   8   6   4   2

LIBRARY OF CONGRESS CATALOGING-IN-PUBLICATION DATA
Rovetch, Lissa   Cora and the elephants / story by Lissa ;
art by Martha Weston and Lissa.   p.   cm.
Summary: Cora, a castaway child who was adopted and raised by
African elephants, persuades her elephant mother and father to
travel with her to San Francisco in search of her roots.
ISBN 0-670-84335-0
[1. Elephants — Fiction.   2. San Francisco — Fiction.]   I. Weston,
Martha, ill.   II. Title.
PZ7.R784Co   1995   [E] — dc20   94-9153   CIP   AC

Printed in China
Set in Carnase

C ora lived with a family of elephants in Africa. She took baths in the watering hole. She ran barefoot on the sun-warmed sand. And she ate fresh fruit from the baobab tree. It was a wonderful life . . . except for one thing.

Cora could not remember how she'd gotten
there in the first place. The older she got, the more
curious she became. So one day she set out to get
some answers.

"Mommy," said Cora. "What was I like as a
baby?"

"Well," said Ophelia, "you were small, dear. And pink."

"Yes, very pink," said Edward.

"And isn't there anything else you'd like to tell me?" asked Cora.

"That we love you very much," said Ophelia. "Now, let's go swat some flies at the watering hole."

The next day, Edward and Ophelia had a talk.

"She's starting to ask questions," said Ophelia. "What are we going to do?"

"We have no other choice, my sweet love-bird," said Edward. "We must finally tell her the truth."

So, when Cora came home for tea, they told her a remarkable story.

"Ophelia and I used to watch boats sailing on the sea," said Edward. "We spent hours guessing what kinds of treasures they might be carrying. Ophelia talked about jewels and gold. And I dreamed of glorious foods."

"Sometimes we found things washed up on the shore," said Ophelia. "An old shoe, a fishing net, or, if we were lucky, a book."

"But one surprising morning we found a real treasure. It was you, Cora dear, a beautiful baby girl. You were tired and red from the African sun. So we scooped you up, tucked you in bed, and gave you cool coconut milk."

Cora was amazed. This was much more exciting than anything else she had ever imagined. "Where did I come from?" she asked. "Where did I live before?"

"All we could find was this tag on your life preserver," said Edward. "It says, 'Pier 38, San Francisco.'"

Cora went straight to their family globe.

"Here's San Francisco," she said. "Let's go see it!"

Ophelia shook her head and sighed. "Be reasonable, sweet Cora. We'd have to take an airplane to go all that way, and you know we haven't got that kind of money."

The fact of the matter was, the elephants didn't have *any* money. So Cora thanked Edward and Ophelia for saving her life, and didn't mention San Francisco again.

But she held on to that life-preserver tag for days. She took it wherever she went, and walked with her head in the clouds, wondering where she had come from.

Had she lived in a house made of grass or stone? Or in a great golden castle like the one in her fairy tale book?

Cora couldn't think about anything else. She lost all interest in food, and started forgetting things. Everyone grew quite concerned.

Then one day she jumped out of bed. "I've got it!" she cried. "I've thought of a wonderful plan!"

"Well, tell us, sugarplum," said Edward. "Ophelia and I are all ears."

"We'll gather up lots of coconuts," said Cora, "and sell them at the town market. We'll earn plenty of money for our trip!"

Now, Ophelia thought this was a very strange idea. But she loved Cora more than anything, and wanted her to be happy again. "Why not?" she said. "I think this family could use an adventure."

"Get your coconuts! Ten dollars a coconut!"
shouted Edward, who was a natural salesman.

"Sweet and delicious," called Ophelia, already
having more fun than she'd expected.

As soon as the shoppers saw that the sales-
people were elephants, they lined up to buy
coconuts. And by the end of the day, Cora,
Edward, and Ophelia had more than enough
money for their trip.

The airplane ride was thrilling. Edward and
Ophelia loved the peanuts and ginger ale. And Cora
felt just like a kestrel bird soaring through the sky.

When they finally got to San Francisco, a taxi driver pulled up and took them right to the address on the life-preserver tag.

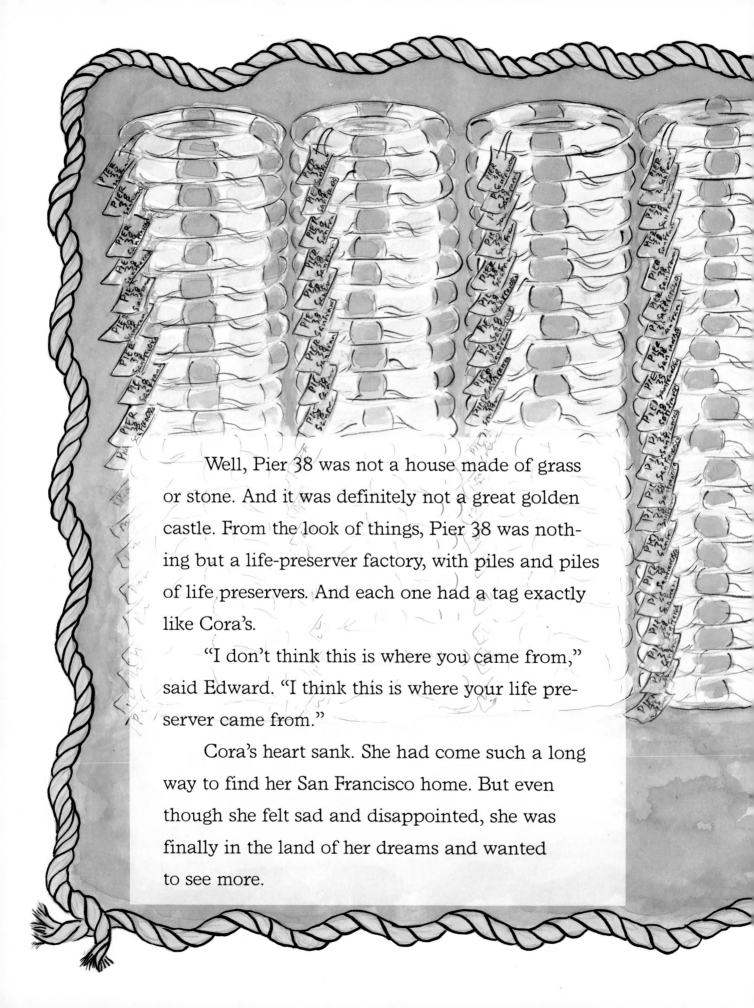

Well, Pier 38 was not a house made of grass or stone. And it was definitely not a great golden castle. From the look of things, Pier 38 was nothing but a life-preserver factory, with piles and piles of life preservers. And each one had a tag exactly like Cora's.

"I don't think this is where you came from," said Edward. "I think this is where your life preserver came from."

Cora's heart sank. She had come such a long way to find her San Francisco home. But even though she felt sad and disappointed, she was finally in the land of her dreams and wanted to see more.

"Greetings!" said Mr. Fishpin, the president of the life-preserver company. "What can I do for you folks today?"

"We're just visiting from Africa," said Edward.

"Africa!" said Mr. Fishpin. "Why, Mrs. Fishpin loves Africa. Say, why don't you folks come home with me? I bet she'd love to meet some real, live elephants."

Mrs. Fishpin made pumpkin stew and mul-
berry pie for dinner.

"You simply must stay with us," she said.
"You can't get home cooking in a silly hotel, and
besides, we can show you the sights."

The Fishpins showed them everything, from
Chinatown to Golden Gate Park. And Cora liked it
so much that she wanted to stay.

Luckily, the Fishpins had a gigantic house.
They filled it with sand, and made a special watering hole in the living room.

Edward, who was always good with numbers,
went to work at the bank. Ophelia became a guide
at the Academy of Sciences Museum. And the
Fishpins made sure that Cora went to the very best
school.

Cora learned all kinds of people things. She had never known there were so many ways to wear her hair. And nobody had ever taught her to do cartwheels or play hopscotch before.

Then one morning, a few months later, Mrs. Fishpin made a special breakfast of German pancakes with lemon butter and applesauce.

"We're so pleased that you've come to live with us," she said. "I just don't know how we ever got along without you."

"We sure do love this big-city life!" said Edward.

But Cora knew how much he hated wearing a suit to work every day, and how hard it was for him to squeeze in and out of the cable cars.

"And we're so pleased that Cora can finally play with people children," said Ophelia.

But Cora knew that Ophelia would rather be talking with real animals in Africa than showing stuffed ones to families in the museum. And Cora had begun to miss her old life. She longed to feel the warm sand on her bare feet. She dreamed of running once again in the open African air.

"You've been so nice to us," Cora told Mrs. Fishpin. "And you're very good at cooking things. But if you don't mind, I think I'd like to go home now."

Edward and Ophelia smiled.

"Now it's your turn to come visit us," said Cora. "We're just across the way from Rhino Rock, right under the baobab tree."

The taxi ride to the airport was very crowded, because Mr. and Mrs. Fishpin insisted on seeing their guests off properly.

"Come again, dear friends," Mrs. Fishpin cried as the airplane flew away.

"And don't forget," called Mr. Fishpin, "our watering hole is your watering hole."

The travelers were happy to be home. They were greeted with hugs and kisses and gifts and cake.

After that, Cora took the long path into town
each week to spend some time doing people things.
But she always went back to the elephants. To
swim and play in the watering hole. To run barefoot on the warm brown sand. To eat fresh fruit
from the baobab tree. And to walk with her family
and friends.